W9-AWN-487

JABBERWOCKY

BY LEWIS CARROLL

WITH ILLUSTRATIONS FROM **THE** *Disney* **ARCHIVES**

DISNEP
PRESS
NEW YORK

Text and illustrations copyright © 1992 Disney Press.
All rights reserved.
No part of this book may be used or reproduced
in any manner whatsoever without the written permission of the publisher.
Printed and bound in the United States of America.
For information address Disney Press,
114 Fifth Avenue, New York, New York 10011.
The stories, characters, and/or incidents
in this publication are entirely fictional.
FIRST EDITION
1   3   5   7   9   10   8   6   4   2

Library of Congress Catalog Card Number: 91-58968
ISBN: 1-56282-245-4/1-56282-246-2 (lib. bdg.)

'Twas brillig, and the slithy toves
  Did gyre and gimble in the wabe;

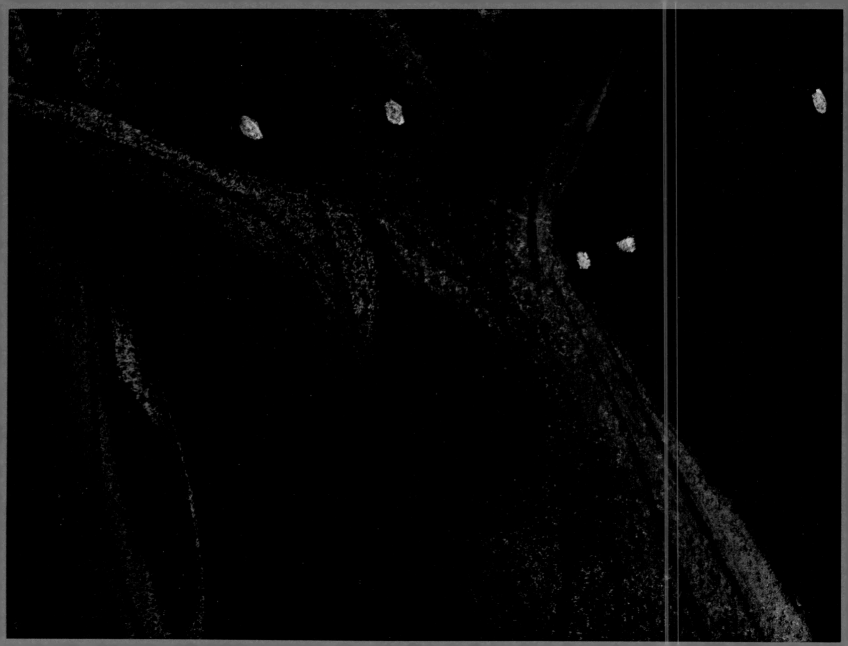

All mimsy were the borogoves,
And the mome raths outgrabe.

"Beware the Jabberwock, my son!
    The jaws that bite, the claws that catch!

Beware the Jubjub bird, and shun
The frumious Bandersnatch!''

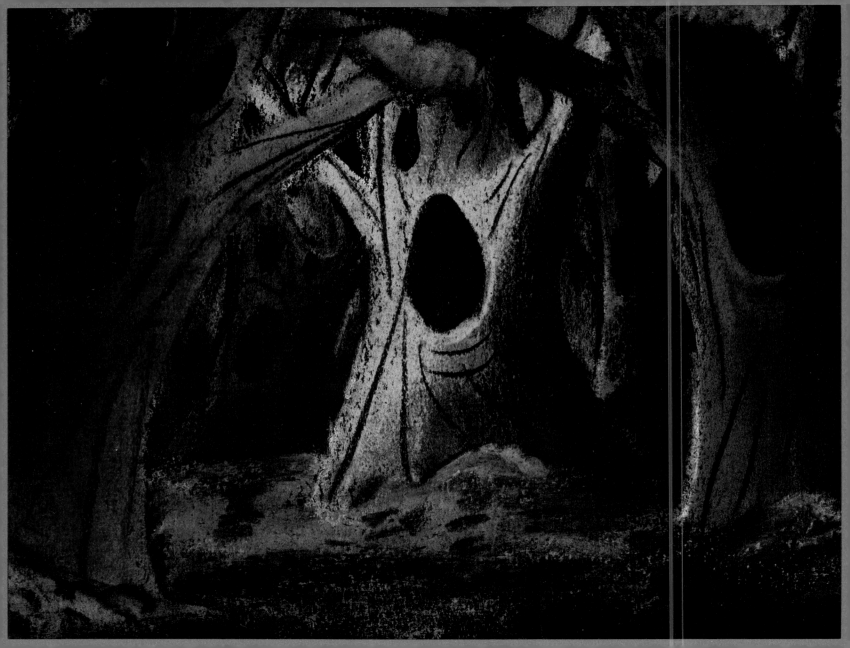

He took his vorpal sword in hand:
   Long time the manxome foe he sought—

So rested he by the Tumtum tree,
And stood awhile in thought.

And as in uffish thought he stood,
    The Jabberwock, with eyes of flame,
Came whiffling through the tulgey wood,
    And burbled as it came!

One, two! One, two! And through and through
The vorpal blade went snicker-snack!

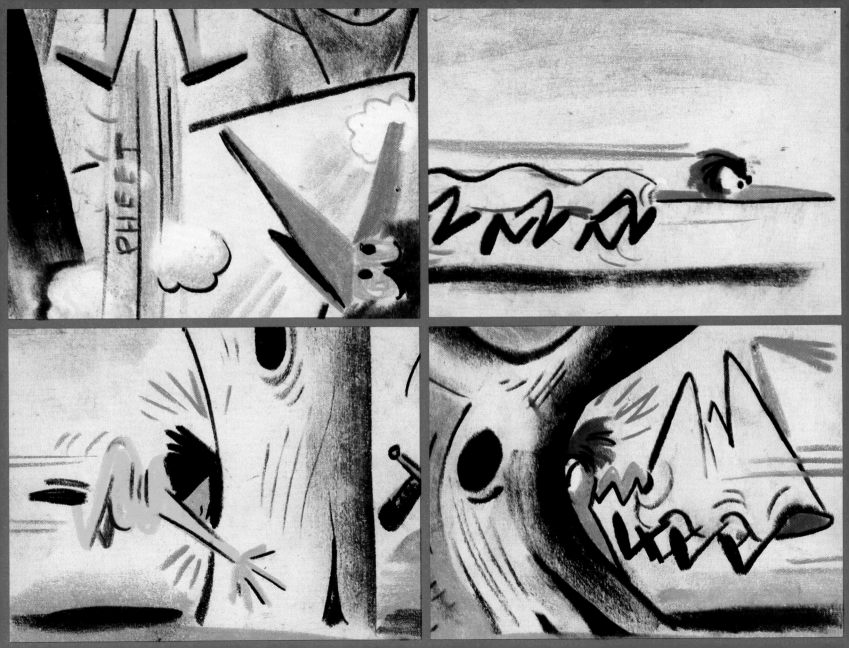

He left it dead, and with its head
He went galumphing back.

"And hast thou slain the Jabberwock?
Come to my arms, my beamish boy!

O frabjous day! Callooh! Callay!''
He chortled in his joy.

'Twas brillig, and the slithy toves
  Did gyre and gimble in the wabe;
All mimsy were the borogoves,
  And the mome raths outgrabe.